FLAKH

# Rise and Shine!

**by Nancy White Carlstrom**

**Pictures by Dominic Catalano**

PC KA

HarperCollins*Publishers*

Rise and Shine!
Text copyright © 1993 by Nancy White Carlstrom
Illustrations copyright © 1993 by Dominic Catalano

Library of Congress Cataloging-in-Publication Data
Carlstrom, Nancy White.
    Rise and shine! / by Nancy White Carlstrom ; pictures by Dominic Catalano.
        p.      cm.
    Summary: A young girl visits all day with the animals on a farm, until it is
time for them to go to sleep and await a new day.
    ISBN 0-06-021451-1. – ISBN 0-06-021452-X (lib. bdg.)
    [1. Domestic animals–Fiction.    2. Stories in rhyme.]    I. Catalano, Dominic,
ill.    II. Title.
PZ8.3.C1948Ri    1993                                                    92-21696
[E]–dc20                                                                      CIP
                                                                              AC

Typography by Christine Kettner
1   2   3   4   5   6   7   8   9   10
❖

First Edition

COCK-A-DOODLE
Cock-a-doodle
Cock-a-doodle-doo!
Sun's up! Sun's up!
And so are you!

Puppy Dog, Puppy Dog,
How will you talk?
With a ruff, ruff, ruff
And a wigwagging walk.

Wooly Lamb, Wooly Lamb,
How will you play?
Friskily, friskily
On this spring day.

Kitty Cat, Kitty Cat,
How will you nap?
Cozy and warm
Curled up on a lap.

What will you wear?
Marmalade fur.
What will you say?
Purr, purr, purr.

Lucky Duck, Lucky Duck,
How will you speak?
With a quack, quack, quack
And a flap of my feet.

Ladybug, Ladybug,
Where will you fly?
Off summer flowers
And into the sky.

Squeaky Mouse, Squeaky Mouse,
How will you eat?
Nibbling, nibbling
On something sweet.

What will you play?
Hide and peek.
What will you say?
Squeak, squeak, squeak.

Piggy Pig, Piggy Pig,
What will you wear?
A curl in my tail
And mud in my hair.

Skitter Squirrel, Skitter Squirrel,
How will you eat?
Crrr-racking, crrr-racking
Nuts with my teeth.

Pokey Snail, Pokey Snail,
How will you talk?
With a shhh, shhh, shhh
On my autumn walk.

Where will you crawl?
Way down low.
How will you move?
Slow, slow, slow.

Nuzzle Horse, Nuzzle Horse,
Where will you go?
To my winter barn
When the cold winds blow.

Lovey Dove, Lovey Dove,
What will you say?
Coo-oo, coo-oo, coo-oo
At the end of the day.

Cuddle Chick, Cuddle Chick,
Where will you rest?
In the fresh warm hay
I make my nest.

What will you say?
Peep, peep, peep.
Until the morning,
Good night! Good sleep.

Cock-a-doodle
Cock-a-doodle
Cock-a-doodle-doo!
Sun's up! Sun's up!

# And so are you!